WHY, OH WHY, WAS I BORN A FLY?

Author

Alex has always had a vivid imagination. As a child she was often described as being in 'Alex's world'. After exploring her fair share of jobs (firefighting, modelling, childcare, estate agency... the list goes on) she is pleased to be putting her 'whizzy' brain (in the words of her parents') to use and concentrating on writing children's books, alongside being a mummy to her three children.

WHY, OH WHY, WAS I BORN A FLY? is Alex's third book following on from her Award-nominated book: WHY, OH WHY, AM I A CROCODILE? and Award-winning book: INSECTS, BUGS & ROCK 'n' ROLL.

WHY, OH WHY, WAS I BORN A FLY?

For my amazing mum and dad
(For putting up with my 'whizzy' brain over the years)

Written by:
Alex Brooks

Illustrated by:
Claudia Zavala

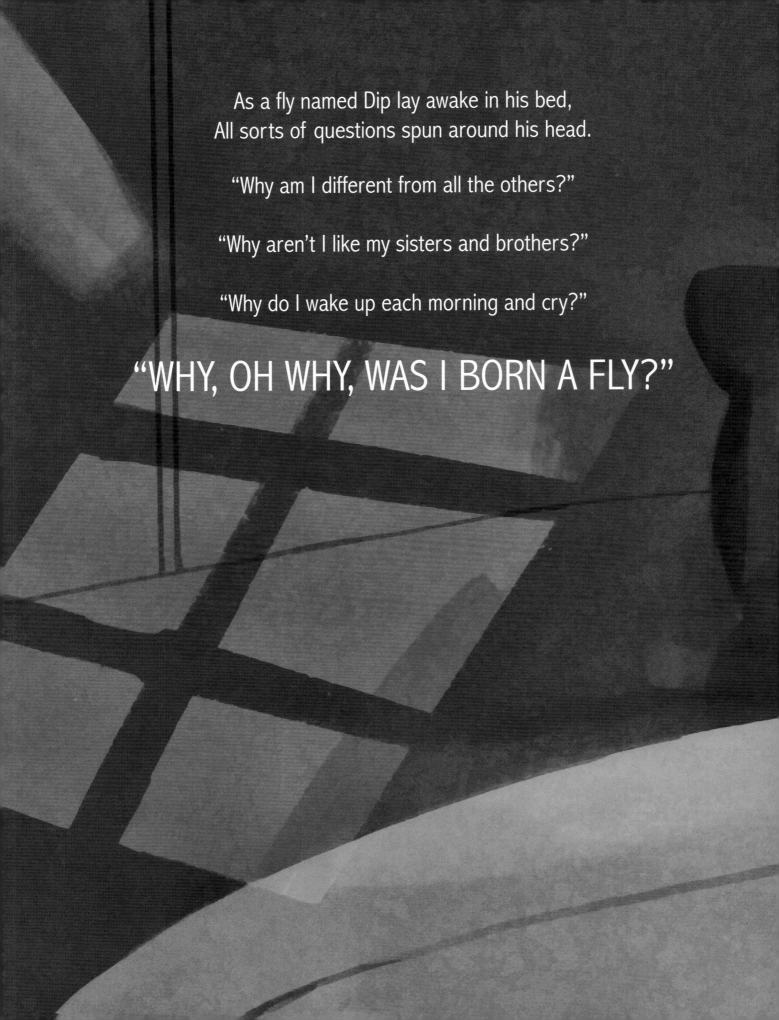

As a fly named Dip lay awake in his bed,
All sorts of questions spun around his head.

"Why am I different from all the others?"

"Why aren't I like my sisters and brothers?"

"Why do I wake up each morning and cry?"

"WHY, OH WHY, WAS I BORN A FLY?"

His siblings would always laugh and tease,
When they'd catch him spying on the bees.

He admired the bees'
magical powers,

Of making honey
and pollinating flowers.

He thought, as a tear rolled from his eye,

"WHY, OH WHY, WAS I BORN A FLY?"

He tried to talk to his mum and dad,
But his dad got angry and his mum got sad.

They'd say,

"He needs to
change his
ways."

He felt alone and unsure what to do,
So, he visited the wisest fly he knew.

"Whatever's the matter?" asked Grandma Fly,
As she dished up her yummy cow pat pie.

"Oh, Grandma dear, what should I do?
No one understands what I'm going through.

I've got the body of a fly, but the mind of a bee,
And I desperately want to feel like me,

I feel so confused while living this lie,

WHY, OH WHY, WAS I BORN A FLY?"

She listened carefully to the words he said,
Then a great idea popped into her head.

She grabbed her wool, began to knit...

...Then handed Dip a **splendid** outfit.

A stripey jumper, yellow and black,
With two holes, for wings, sewn in the back.

Dip pulled on the jumper, feeling shy
But knew it was time to give something a try.

He looked in the mirror with pure delight,
As suddenly everything just felt right.

He said to Grandma, as he gave her a kiss,
"I've been waiting forever to look like this!"

Then he thanked her dearly, waved goodbye,
And full of pride, shot off for the sky.

With his wings spread wide, he flew with ease,
Getting admiring looks from a swarm of bees.

Dip's newfound confidence had him feeling brave,
So he gave them a smile, and they returned a wave.

They beckoned him over to join in their play,
Buzzing and bumbling for the rest of the day.

Joyfully gliding up through the air,

Flower to flower, here and there.

Dip laughed, Dip smiled, Dip felt so free,
And it all made sense, while he was a bee.

As the night drew near, it was time for home,
So, he wriggled and jiggled out of the comb.

But as he took off, he felt something pull,
Looking back in horror at a loose string of wool.

It was a strand of his jumper, stuck to the honey,
(Which the bees were finding terribly funny).

GLUP!

Rapidly unravelling, Dip let out a cry -

"WHY, OH WHY, WAS I BORN A FLY?"

He sobbed all the way to
Grandma's door,
And feeling heartbroken, he
fell to the floor.

"Whatever's the matter?"
asked Grandma Fly,
Dishing up the last of her
signature pie.

"The secret's out, that I'm neither fly nor bee,
Now who will want to be friends with me?"

"My dearest grandchild, can't you see,
True friends don't mind if you're a fly or a bee.

It's not your body, your face or arms,
It's your courage, your kindness
and endless charms.

The reason you're loved
is for what is inside.
What you choose to look like,
is for you to decide."

He listened carefully to
what Grandma said,
And as silence fell,
thoughts filled his head.

Then in the distance they heard a strange sound,
Which got louder and louder and grew all around.

Above the house of Grandma Fly,
An abundance of bees was filling the sky.

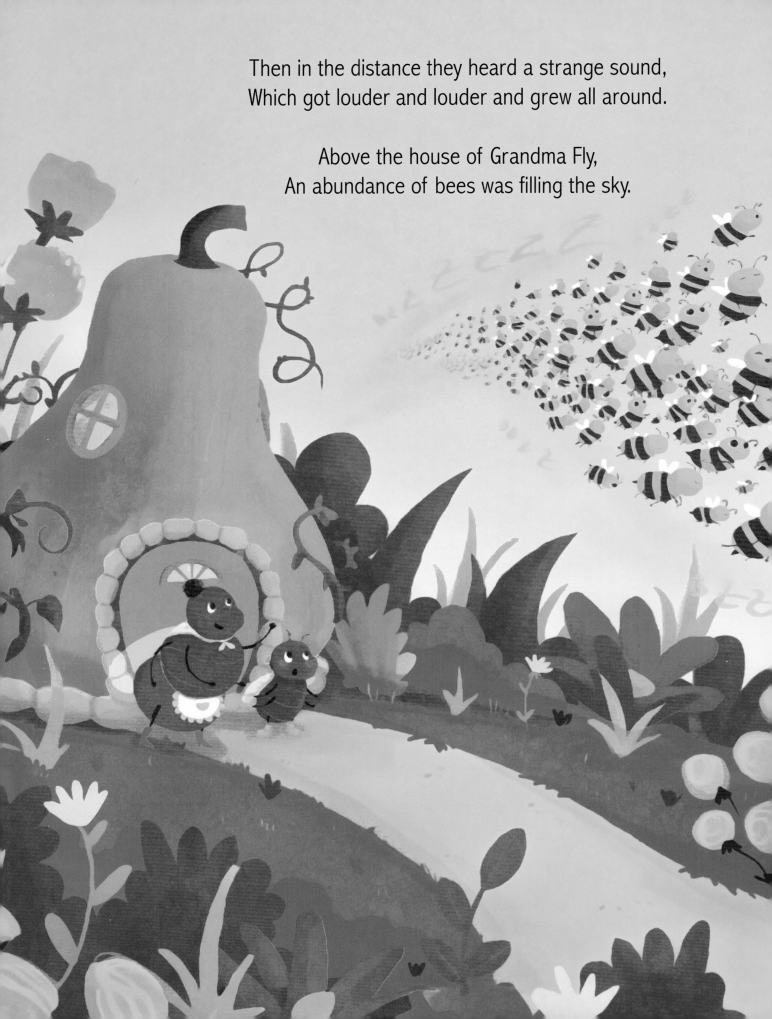

And using the wool from Dip's knitted sweater,
They appeared to be making letter after letter,

Revealing a message, for all to see,
Saying...

You can who want to

"I think it's time to give this a try,"
Said a very excited Grandma Fly.

She gave him a leotard, yellow and black,
With two holes, for wings, sewn in the back.

Dip slipped on the outfit, full of glee,
Then flew outside, for the others to see.

When they saw the transformed Dip appear,

The bees gathered round to clap and to cheer.

Grandma had come up with a perfect solution,
And news travelled fast of Dip's evolution.

Slowly more bugs began to speak out,

Of feelings of loneliness
and self-doubt.

They started travelling from far and wide,
Relieved that they no longer had to hide.

Grandma opened a shop, making
outfits aplenty,
And on the first day alone, she sold
more than twenty.

Each day after that, her
customers doubled,
With masses of insects, all
feeling troubled.

She made shiny red jackets with
spots of black,

Tops with bright patterned
wings on the back.

Suits with eight legs,

Hats with antennae,

And togs for a bee who felt like a fly.

Although life for Dip was by no means a doddle,
He had somehow become the perfect role model.

Now admired by his parents, sisters and brothers,
And cherished for his courage and helping others.

So, if you feel like Dip, speak out, be free,
As you can be whoever you want to be.